STALKED BY THE EXECUTIVE

EMMA BRAY

CHAPTER
ONE

Marcus

I STRIDE INTO LE CINQ, scanning the elegant dining room. I have a table waiting on standby whenever I require it. My company sees to it that I never have to wait.

Just one of the many perks of being a billionaire executive. But with my status comes long nights and stress. I cherish these little breaks I take here.

My gaze finally settles on a young brunette waitress clearing a table in the corner, and I go completely still. I've never seen her in here before. She must be knew.

I take in her petite form, the way her skirt hugs her

shapely hips, the way her button-up blouse clings to the curves of her breasts.

And holy fuck, her face. She has striking blue eyes and an innocent smile. The body of a siren, the face of an angel.

I swallow thickly, my erection instant and throbbing. The mere sight of a woman has never had me so hard-up before.

What is it about this girl?

It's like I have tunnel vision. All I see is her as I made my way toward her, like I'm in a trance.

I don't even see the passing waiter, and when I bump into him, I send the contents of a glass tumbling onto the pretty little waitress's crisp white blouse.

"Fuck, I'm so sorry." The words tumble from my lips as I grasp her arms, our eyes locking. I try not to notice the way the liquid soaks up her white blouse, making the material nearly translucent. A spark of electricity crackles between us and a flush creeps up her delicate neck.

She attempts to brush off my apology. "Please don't worry. It was just an accident."

I remove my suit coat and wrap it around her, my knuckles grazing the swell of her breasts. All I can think about is covering her before other male eyes see what I saw.

She's *mine*.

I don't know why I'm suddenly so possessive of this girl, but I am. I don't want anyone else looking at her. No one else can touch her. Only me.

"It was my carelessness. Let me make it up to you." I stare into her pretty blue eyes and fight back a groan.

Her rosebud lips part. "That won't be necessary."

I slide my fingers under her chin, tilting her face up to mine, marveling at how petal soft her skin is. She's like a porcelain doll. So beautiful. So fragile. And I find myself just wanting to take her home with me and lock her up. "Nonsense. I insist you join me for dinner...on me, of course."

Her cheeks flame as she struggles to form a response. She's clearly rattled, though whether from fear or desire I can't yet tell.

"I'm sorry. I'm on the clock, Sir."

"I know the manager. He will make an exception at my request," I insist.

After a long moment, she relents with a whispered, "Alright."

Triumph surges through me.

"Excellent. I'm Marcus Wellington." I take her hand and brush my lips across her knuckles.

"Charlotte Turner." A shiver runs through her delicate frame as she utters her name.

I smile, tightening my grip on her hand. "It's a pleasure to meet you, Charlotte."

Our gazes remain locked, a silent promise of what's to come passing between us. I've found my obsession, and there's no turning back now.

She's *mine*.

I lead Charlotte to my usual table, pulling out her chair for her. She sits, smoothing her skirt over her thighs. I take the seat across from her, studying her openly.

In the soft light of the restaurant, she's even lovelier than I first noticed. Full lips, high cheekbones, and wide blue eyes that hold a hint of innocence despite her obvious intelligence.

A wave of possessiveness washes over me. I want to be the one to shatter that innocence, to expose the wanton creature she's destined to become under my tutelage.

"Have you worked here long?" I ask, struggling to keep my tone casual. I already know she hasn't. I'd definitely have noticed her. I signal the waiter for a bottle of wine.

"Today is my first day." She ducks her head, a blush staining her cheeks. "I'm trying to pay for school."

"Ah, so you're a student then. Studying what, may I ask?"

"Literature." She meets my gaze again, her eyes bright. "I want to be a writer."

"How ambitious." I pour her a glass of wine and lift my own. "To your dreams, Charlotte Turner."

"Thank you." She smiles, the warmth in her expression setting my blood aflame. "And you, Mr. Wellington? What is it you do?"

I stare at her a minute. It's refreshing to meet someone who doesn't know who I am. It's clear by her innocent gaze that she truly doesn't know.

"Please, call me Marcus." I take a generous swallow of wine, the bitter tang a poor substitute for the taste I crave. "I'm in acquisitions. My company seeks out valuable assets and makes them our own."

Her lips part on a soft intake of breath, and I picture them swollen from our kisses, bruised from the ferocity of my possession.

"That sounds...challenging." She fidgets with her napkin, her knuckles white.

I reach across the table to still her hands, stroking my thumbs over her knuckles. "Do I make you nervous, Charlotte?"

She pulls away sharply, panic flaring in her eyes. "I'm sorry, Mr. Wellington, but I should return to my work."

My grip on her tightens, desire churning in my gut. She'll not escape me so easily. I have her now, and I won't let go.

I swallow the urge to drag her into my arms and

kiss the defiance from her lips. *No, I mustn't frighten her.*

"Forgive me," I say softly. "I didn't mean to alarm you." I release her hands and lean back, affecting a casual air. "It seems I've overstepped. Allow me to make it up to you."

She hesitates, watching me warily. "How do you mean?"

"Come work for me." The words spill from my lips before I can stop them. "You're too intelligent and ambitious to waste your potential waiting tables. Be my personal secretary. I'll double your salary, give you opportunities to advance. You can pursue your dreams on your own time."

I hold my breath, praying I haven't revealed too much, as she considers my offer. Her eyes narrow, and for one heart-stopping moment, I'm certain she sees through my facade.

Then she smiles, relief and joy transforming her features, and I breathe again. "I don't know what to say. That's incredibly generous of you."

"Generosity has nothing to do with it." I return her smile, hiding my triumph. "I'm investing in talent. Do we have a deal?"

"Yes!" She laughs, the sound like music to my ears. "When do I start?"

"Tomorrow." I stand and draw several bills from my

wallet, more than enough to cover her wages for the week. "Go home. Consider this your first payment."

"But—"

"No arguments." I press the money into her hand and close her fingers around the crisp notes. "I'll have a car pick you up at 8 am. We have a great deal of work ahead of us, Charlotte."

"I look forward to it." Her cheeks flush becomingly as she meets my gaze. "Thank you again...Marcus."

"The pleasure is mine." I bring her hand to my lips, kissing her knuckles once more and reveling in her shiver. "Until tomorrow, my dear."

With that, I take my leave, hunger and anticipation quickening my steps into the night. I pull out my cell phone and call my head of security. He answers on the first ring as always. "Yes, boss?"

"Get me everything you can on Charlotte Turner."

***

The next morning, Charlotte arrives promptly at 8 am. I greet her myself, leading her to the spacious office that will now be hers.

"I wasn't expecting this," she says, eyes wide as she takes in the view of the city from the floor-to-ceiling windows. "It's beautiful."

"Only the best for my personal assistant." I place a hand at the small of her back, gratified by her responsive shiver. "Shall we get started?"

She nods, turning to face me with a smile. "What would you like me to do first?"

I steeple my fingers, affecting a thoughtful pose. "The charity gala my company hosts annually is coming up next month. I would like for you to help organize the event. You'll have full control over which charities and organizations we sponsor. Does that sound like a good start?"

"Yes, absolutely!" Excitement animates her expression, blue eyes glowing. "Thank you so much for this opportunity, Marcus. I won't let you down."

"I know you won't." Unable to resist, I reach out and tuck a stray lock of hair behind her ear. She stills at my touch, cheeks flushing, and I thrill at her involuntary response.

Mine.

The possessive thought comes unbidden, but I don't fight it. Charlotte Turner belongs to me now, in all the ways that matter. I only need to make her realize that truth for herself.

Throughout the day, I watch Charlotte from the shadows of my office as she settles into her new role. She moves with purpose and poise, greeting coworkers and fielding calls with confidence. But there are moments when she pauses, tucking a stray lock of hair behind her ear or chewing on her lower lip, that betray her nerves.

"Did you need something, Mr. Wellington?"

Charlotte's question startles me from my thoughts. She stands in the doorway of my office, a stack of files clutched to her chest and a quizzical expression on her face.

"Just observing," I reply smoothly. "Making sure you have everything you need to get started."

"I belive I have everything under control." Her chin lifts a fraction, and I supress a smile.

"Duly noted." I pin her in place with a smoldering look, watching with satisfaction as a blush stains her cheeks. "Thank you, Charlotte. I'll be sure to let you know if I need anything...personal."

The emphasis is slight, and I could shook myself when Charlotte flushes deeper, blue eyes widening with something akin to panic. The stack of files tumble to the floor in a flurry of papers.

I bend to help her pick them up.

"I'm so sorry," she apologies, her face flaming.

"Sweetheart, there's nothing to be sorry for," I tell her gently.

Her eyes snap up to me at the endearment, her lips parting. My cock instantly grows to full mast, and I discreetly turn away from her to adjust myself as I rise.

I feel Charlotte's gaze on me like a physical caress, her uncertainty and curiosity a heady combination. I'm acutely aware of her every movement, my senses attuned to her in a way that borders on obsession.

When she rises from the floor, I track her progress with a hooded gaze. The sway of her hips and rustle of her skirt quicken my pulse, arousal and possessiveness warring for dominance. I want to mark her, *claim* her, devour her whole.

By the time Charlotte returns to her desk, composure regained, I've conjured a dozen fantasies of how I'll make her mine.

And she *will* be mine.

CHAPTER
TWO

Marcus

I WAIT until Charlotte leaves for her night class before making my way to her apartment. My heart pounds as I slip inside, the familiar scent of her perfume lingering in the air.

I shouldn't be here. This is a violation of her privacy, but the need to be close to her consumes me. I can't stay away.

In her bedroom, I run my fingers over the softness of her comforter, imagining her delicate body writhing beneath me. I grip the headboard, steadying myself against the surge of desire rippling through my veins.

Fuck, I want her. The ache is almost too much to bear.

In the kitchen, I find a glass and pour myself a drink. The burn of the whiskey does little to ease the fire raging inside me. I slam the glass on the counter, the crystal shattering under my grip.

Shit. I take a deep breath, forcing myself to stay in control. I have to be careful. One wrong move and I could lose her forever.

I clean up the broken glass and head for the door. As much as it pains me to leave, I have to go before she returns. But I'll be back.

Charlotte is *mine.* She just doesn't know it yet.

I return to Charlotte's apartment the next night, driven by an insatiable hunger. My heart pounds as I slip inside, the thrill of trespassing fueling my desire.

In her bedroom, I search through her lingerie drawer until I find a pair of lace panties. *She wore these.* Her scent lingers on the soft fabric, intoxicating me.

I press the panties to my face, breathing her in. "Charlotte," I groan, my cock twitching. I imagine her delicate sex, pink and glistening, barely concealed by this scrap of lace.

Fuck, I'm so hard for her. I ache to thrust deep

inside her tight heat, marking her, claiming her, ravaging her sweet body until she screams my name.

I grip the panties tighter, stroking myself. I'm close, so close.

In my mind, Charlotte is here with me. Naked. Vulnerable. Begging for release.

"Please," she cries. "I need you, Marcus."

Her imagined plea sends me over the edge. I come with a shout, coating the panties in hot spurts of cum. The intensity leaves me trembling, but still wanting more.

I'll never have enough of her. She is my addiction, my obsession, my everything.

And one day, she will be mine.

———

Back at the office, I watch Charlotte's every move, my eyes fixated on her petite frame and flowing brunette hair.

Desire pools in my gut as Charlotte bends over a table, her skirt riding up to reveal smooth thighs. I imagine those legs wrapped around my waist, drawing me deeper inside her.

She glances up, catching me staring. A blush stains her cheeks, but she doesn't look away.

Heat flares in her eyes, igniting my hunger. She wants this as much as I do. She's just afraid to admit it.

I want to stalk toward her, pin her against the table. Tell her she drives me fucking crazy.

She would tremble, her breathing becoming ragged.

I imagine a soft moan escaping her lips, her resistance crumbling.

Fuuuuck.

I rush into the bathroom, my cock straining against my zipper.

One imagined touch. That's all it takes to unravel my control.

I rip open my pants, fisting my erection. I'm so hard it hurts, throbbing with need.

In my mind, I see Charlotte on her knees before me.

"Please me," I demand.

She gazes up at me, lips parted, ready to take me deep.

With a groan, I thrust into her mouth, tangling my hands in her hair. She takes me eagerly, hollowing her cheeks as she sucks me in.

The fantasy is so vivid, I can almost feel the glide of her tongue, the warmth of her mouth. Pressure builds at the base of my spine, spiking sharply.

I'm close. So close.

"Look at me," I order. Charlotte's eyes meet mine, filled with desire, devotion and submission.

That's my undoing. I come with a shout, coating my fist in hot spurts of cum.

Breathless, I lean against the wall. I'm momentarily relieved, but it's not enough. I'm still aching because it's not *her*.

I won't be satisfied until Charlotte is mine completely.

I clean myself up and return to my desk, hunger gnawing at my insides.

Charlotte walks by, oblivious, her hips swaying. I stare at the curve of her ass, heat pooling in my groin again.

Christ, I'm insatiable where she's concerned. I want to possess her, dominate her, break her, and mold her to my will.

She'll fight me at first, but I'll show her pleasure like she's never known. Charlotte will come to crave my touch the way I crave hers. She'll beg to serve me, to please me.

And she will. Becuase she's such a good girl.

Charlotte glances over, a question marring her pretty face. I school my expression into one of indifference and look away.

She bends over, and I peak another glance at her, my cock rocketing to full mast again when I see the peak of her lacy white panties from underneath her skirt.

Jesus, does she know? No, my little Charlotte is so innocent, she has no clue her pretty little panty-clad pussy is taunting her boss like this.

My breathing becomes ragged at I stare at her mound. It's just enough to tease and entire. I rush to the bathroom again. No sooner am I behind closed door do I have my aching cock in my fist again. My movements are desperate and urgent as I reach the peak of my pleasure, my release a temporary relief from my insatiable desire.

I pump into my fist, Charlotte's name a ragged cry on my lips. The coil of tension in my groin snaps, pleasure flooding my senses. I come in hot spurts, coating my hand and the floor of the bathroom once more.

My legs tremble as I brace myself against the wall, chest heaving. The haze of lust clears, leaving shame and self-loathing in its wake.

What the hell am I doing? This obsession with Charlotte has turned me into a horny teenaged boy who can't control his nut.

I clean up my mess with shaking hands, cursing under my breath. *Get a grip, Marcus.*

I splash cold water on my face, looking at the stranger in the mirror. How did I come to this? When did I lose control?

You didn't lose control. You handed it to Charlotte the moment you became obsessed.

The thought fills me with anger. *I'm* in control, always in control.

But even as I tell myself that, I know it's a lie. Charlotte has me twisted around her little finger, and she doesn't even know it.

———

I emerge from the bathroom to find Charlotte typing at her desk, brows furrowed in concentration. She looks up and smiles at me, warmth flooding her blue eyes.

"Everything okay, Mr. Wellington?"

The concern in her voice makes me ache. She's always so solicitous, so caring. If only she knew the effect she has on me.

"Fine," I say brusquely. "Get back to work."

Charlotte's smile fades, and I feel a stab of guilt. I shouldn't take out my frustration on her. It isn't her fault I can't control myself.

I retreat to my office and close the door, needing distance from her intoxicating presence. But it's no use. No matter how far apart we are, Charlotte is always in my mind, refusing to leave me be.

This obsession will destroy me if I don't find a way to sate it.

Control. I have to maintain control.

But how can I when every thought, every waking

moment is filled with Charlotte? I can't escape this craving, this bone-deep need to possess her, own her, mark her as mine.

I bury my head in my hands, my body tight with tension. I want to hurt something, destroy something, expend this restless energy that threatens to overwhelm me.

If I don't find release soon, I won't be able to stop myself from taking Charlotte, propriety and consent be damned. I'll throw her down, rip that prim skirt away, and bury myself inside her little virgin cunt until she screams my name.

Becuase I don't know how I know, but I just *know* she's got a perfect little untapped pussy. No man in his right mind would ever let her go if he got inside her. I growl now just thinking of another man touching her.

No one will ever touch her. No one but *me*. I'll make sure of that.

The office is empty now, the silence broken only by the ticking of the clock.

But in my mind, Charlotte's soft cries and pleas for mercy echo on a loop. I close my eyes and picture her bound and trembling before me, her flawless skin marked with the imprint of my hands.

Mine. All mine.

The thought sends a surge of heat through my

veins. I grip the arms of my chair, the leather creaking under my hands.

I could end this torture with a single phone call. Charlotte would come if I summoned her. She wouldn't dare refuse me.

My fingers flex around the phone, itching to make that call. Every second we're apart is agony. I need her here, need to sink into the heat of her body and erase the distance between us.

No. Not yet.

I release the phone and take a deep, steadying breath. *Patience. I have to be patient.*

When I claim Charlotte, it will be forever. There can be no hesitation, no room for doubt or second thoughts. She has to be ready to give herself to me fully, as I will give myself to her.

We belong to each other, two halves of the same whole. It's only a matter of time before Charlotte accepts her fate.

I lean back again and smile up at the ceiling, imagining the day when Charlotte finally comes to me of her own accord, ready to accept both damnation and salvation in my arms.

The waiting will make that victory all the sweeter. Charlotte is already mine. Now I just have to help her realize that inescapable truth.

CHAPTER
THREE

Charlotte

THIS JOB HAS BEEN A GODSEND. I'll admit. I was irritated when my first day on my new waitressing job someone spilled something on me.

But it has turned out to be the best thing that's ever happened to me. With the money I make working for Marcus, I'm able to pay for my night classes. Not that I technically need a degree to keep writing. I just want one, I guess.

Marcus tasks me with organizing files and scheduling meetings, menial jobs that allow us to work side by side for hours. At first, we chat casually about hobbies and interests, building an easy rapport. But soon, our conversations turn personal.

One day, Marcus confesses his greatest fear is dying alone, unloved and uncared for. The admission catches me off guard, revealing a vulnerability I never expected. I reach out, squeezing his hand. "That won't happen."

He looks up, surprise flickering in his eyes. Then he smiles, a soft, genuine smile that makes my heart stutter. "Thank you, Charlotte. Your kindness means a lot."

Heat infuses my cheeks. I duck my head, embarrassed by the strength of my reaction. I'm falling for him, hard and fast. The realization terrifies me. Marcus is my boss, which means he's off-limits. If we pursue a relationship, it could end in disaster.

Yet when I'm with him, I feel happier than I have in years. He understands me in a way no one else does. He accepts me, flaws and all. I've never met anyone who challenges and inspires me the way Marcus does.

I know it's wrong to care for him like this. But my heart refuses to listen to reason. Every smile, every touch, every glimpse into his complicated soul only deepens my feelings. I'm caught in a riptide, being pulled under with no chance of escape. All I can do is brace myself for what's to come.

My emotions war within me, desire and duty locked

in a battle of wills. I want to give in to this spark between us, consequences be damned. I want to lose myself in his embrace and savor the passion I know we could share.

But I can't. I have to stay strong and protect my heart. No matter how badly it hurts. And if working closely with Marcus Wellington ignites a fire inside me, one I'm powerless to extinguish, so be it. I'll simply have to endure the flames.

***

I'm beat as I return home. I headed straight for class after work today, and all I want to do is take a hot shower and crash into bed.

But something isn't right. I know it as soon as I step into my apartment. I don't know how I know, but I *know*. The apartment is eerily silent.

My heart rate ticks up.

My keys jangle in the lock, and the door creaks open. I walk into my apartment cautiously.

But I don't see anything wrong. Everything looks exactly as it should.

I glance toward the bedroom.

I walk slowly toward it. Everything looks fine in here too, except...

I glance at my cracked dresser door. My panty drawer.

Bile rises in my throat I make my way over to the

drawer. A quick glance inside shows a pair of my panties missing.

Oh my god, someone was here. And they stole a pair of my panties.

I force myself to breathe in and out. And then I suddenly feel like I'm being watched.

Icy terror washes over me. *I'm not alone.*

Someone is here.

I spin around, scanning the room. Heart seized in my chest, I peer into the shadows, waiting, listening. Silence envelops me, thick and suffocating. The air itself seems threatening.

Any second, he could emerge. Reach out with rough, calloused hands. Drag me into the darkness.

I have to get out. *Now.*

I rush for the front door, nearly tripping in my haste. My hands fumble with the lock, refusing to turn. Panic rises in my throat. Almost there...

The door bursts open. I scream.

A man stands in the doorway, tall and broad-shouldered, his features obscured by the dim light of the hallway.

"Charlotte? Are you alright?" It's Marcus. I recognize his voice, laced with concern.

I stumble back, clutching at the wall. My chest heaves as I struggle for air.

He steps forward, hands raised in a placating gesture.

I don't even ask what he's doing here. I just throw myself in his arms in relief. "Someone was in my apartment. They stole a pair of my panties."

Marcus shushes me and strokes a hand over my hair. "It's okay. I'm here now."

"You shouldn't be alone right now." His tone brooks no argument. "Come home with me tonight."

Marcus shifts, leaning against the wall. He exudes a quiet confidence and strength. Perhaps it's foolish, but I feel safer with him, so I don't even hesitate to accept his proposal.

Marcus steps closer, radiating heat and a spicy cologne. My senses heighten at his nearness. "How did you come to be here?"

"I happened to be in the area, and call it a sixth sense, but you were just on my mind. Thought I'd check on you." His eyes darken.

I stare at the floor, at the scuffs on my shoes. An uneasy feeling coils in my gut as the weight of his gaze bores into me.

"Charlotte." His voice drops, rough and intimate.

I look up without thinking. Our eyes meet, and my breath catches.

Heat and hunger blaze in his eyes. His pupils are blown wide, lips parted. The air between us seems to shimmer with electricity.

"Come on. It's late, and we have to work tomorrow. I have a spare bedroom you can stay in."

I follow him because what else can I do?

————

Marcus

I stalk down the hallway, pulse pounding in my veins. She almost caught me last night. It was a quick save to "just so happen" to show up at her door and present myself as her savior instead of being found out as her villain.

Her classes must have ended early. Either that or I got so wrapped up in my fantasies that time ran away from me.

It was more likely the latter. I'm lucky I was able to sneak out of her bedroom fire escape before she caught me.

But damn it, I didn't close her dresser drawer all the way in my haste.

I'll have to be more careful in the future.

I don't know how the fuck I kept my hands off her last night. She was in my house, within reach.

I didn't sleep a wink. I jacked off obsessively, so much so that I'm surprised there's still any cum left in my body.

But apparently there is because my cock is twitching and rising again at the thought of her.

I drag a hand over his face, struggling for control. Now is not the time to act on impulse. Last night was proof enough of that. I need to be careful, patient.

I scowl down at my pants as if my cock is personally to blame for all my troubles. It's making an obscene tent in my pants.

Motherfucker.

I stalk to my executive bathroom, my breathing ragged. The craving burns through my blood, fueled by the lacy scrap of fabric in my pocket.

I locks the door behind me and pulls out the stolen panties, clutching the delicate material in my fist. I close my eyes and inhale her scent, musk and jasmine and something uniquely Charlotte.

A groan rumbles in my chest as I palm the front of my trousers. My erection strains against the expensive wool, aching for release.

With trembling fingers, I unzip my fly and draw out my cock. It jerks in my grip as I rub the panties over the sensitive head, slick precum staining the lace.

I stuff the panties back in my pocket, not wanting to chance making a mess on them until I've stolen another pair.

Jesus, I'm sick. *Obsessed.*

"Charlotte," I rasp, fist tightening around my length. I imagine her on her knees before me, full lips parted, eyes dark with desire as—

A sharp cry escapes me as pleasure spikes through my body. My climax crashes over me in waves, Charlotte's name a broken moan on his lips as I start to come...

———

Charlotte

I knock softly on the bathroom door. "Marcus? Are you okay in there?"

No response. Unease trickles down my spine. Something isn't right.

I push the door open and freeze in shock. Marcus stands at the sink, his back to me. His arm is moving a mile a minute, and then I think I hear my name come from his lips in a rasp.

And then he groans, long and deep as white stuff starts shooting from his hard flesh.

He opens his eyes. They're dark with desire as they meet mine. I see the surprise light in them before more liquid comes spurting out of him.

I stare at his spasming flesh. It seems like it's never going to stop. My mouth falls open, and I can't look away.

My eyes drop to the floor stained with an unfamiliar fluid. I stare at it, confusion and disbelief warring in my mind, until understanding dawns.

A flush creeps up my neck as I realize what Marcus was doing.

I should feel disgusted, but I'm not. Instead, heat pools low in my belly, a coil of arousal I don't want to acknowledge.

Marcus's chest is heaving up and down, his eyes hooded and expression unreadable. We stare at each other, the tension thick between us, waiting to see who will break first.

"Charlotte." My name is a ragged whisper from his lips. "I can explain."

But no explanation is needed.

Marcus takes a step toward me, eyes burning into mine. I stand frozen, caught in his thrall, heart pounding as he slowly advances.

"Charlotte." His voice is rough velvet, stroking over my skin.

I duck my head in embarrassment and bolt for the door, heart in my throat.

I don't know how I'm ever going to be able to look him in the eye again.

CHAPTER
FOUR

Charlotte

MY HANDS TREMBLE as I walk into Wellington Tower for another day as Mr. Wellington's personal secretary. But all I can think about his Marcus in bathroom, fisting his hard flesh, the look in his eyes.

I flush, my panties getting wet just thinking about it.

The marble lobby dwarfs me, all sharp edges and cold gleam. My heels click on the floor, echoing in the cavernous space.

When the elevator doors slide open, I find Marcus waiting inside. His gaze rakes over me, dark eyes lingering on my curves before meeting my eyes. A shiver runs down my spine at the intensity in his stare.

"Ms. Turner, welcome." His voice is a low purr, silky and smooth. He acts completely unaffected by what I witnessed yesterday. But maybe that's for the best, that we pretend it didn't even happen.

"Thank you, Mr. Wellington." I duck my head, hiding the blush staining my cheeks.

He presses the button for the top floor. We ascend in silence, the air crackling with tension. I cling to the railing, acutely aware of his towering presence beside me.

When the doors open again, he places a hand on my lower back, guiding me out. "I trust you had a good night, Charlotte."

A thrill runs through me at his touch, his use of my first name. "Yes, sir."

He tsks at me. "Marcus, please. No need to stand on ceremony. We're friends first and foremost, aren't we?"

I smile up at him tentatively. "Marcus."

The corners of his eyes crinkle with his genuine smile, and I can't help but think that he's the most handsome man I've ever seen.

And then the image of his cock flashes through my mind, and my face heats.

My heart pounds as I follow him into his office. This job is my salvation, a chance to turn my life around. So what if I saw his dick? So what if it was huge and thick and girthy and swollen? So what if it makes me press my thighs together even now?

We go through the day like usual. Neither of us speaks about what I witnessed yesterday, but it is definitely the elephant in the room.

Finally, at the end of the day, Marcus leans back against his desk, watching me with an unreadable expression. I fidget under the weight of his gaze, heat flooding my cheeks. His eyes darken, pupils dilating with what looks like desire.

"You should head home," he says, voice rough. "It's getting late."

I nod, clutching the folder in my hands like a shield. "Of course. I'll see you tomorrow."

As I turn to leave, Marcus catches my wrist. His fingers wrap around my arm, hot against my skin, sending a jolt of electricity through me. I freeze in place, heartbeat quickening.

"Charlotte." My name is a husky whisper on his lips. "I can't stop thinking about you."

A shiver races down my spine at his admission. I stare up at him, caught in the intensity of his stare. He takes a step closer, eyes flickering to my mouth. I suck in a sharp breath, anticipation and panic warring within me.

"Ever since that first day I saw you at the restaurant, I haven't been able to focus on anything else." His thumb strokes along the inside of my wrist, a feather-light caress that makes me tremble. "I want you, Charlotte. In a way I've never wanted anyone before."

My heart pounds against my ribs like a wild thing trying to break free. "Marcus, we can't—"

"To hell with propriety. Why do you think I gave you this job? I don't need a fucking secretary. I need you. Why do you think I was jacking off like a rabid animal yesterday? It was because of you, Charlotte," he growls as pulls me flush against him, one hand gripping my hip. I gasp at the feel of his hard body pressed against mine, heat and desire kindling low in my belly. "I don't care about rules or boundaries anymore. All I care about is you."

His eyes blaze into mine, dark with a hunger that mirrors my own. My resolve cracks and crumbles, swept away by a tidal wave of passion.

Me? He was doing that because of *me*? Heat floods me as I realize I *like* that I'm the one who made him that way.

I reach up and twine my arms around his neck, surrendering to the flames. When his mouth claims mine, hot and demanding, I melt into his embrace. There's no turning back now. We've fallen too far to escape this raging inferno consuming us both.

Marcus kisses like he does everything else—with single-minded intensity and ruthless control. His hands roam my body, stroking along my sides and hips before sliding up to cup my breasts. I arch into his touch with a soft moan, desire coiling tight within me.

When he finally releases my mouth, we're both breathless. "I want to know everything about you," he rasps, eyes dark and hungry. "Your hopes, your dreams, your deepest secrets."

His gaze burns into me, stripping away my defenses. I swallow hard, trembling in his arms. "There's not much to tell."

"I don't believe that." He brushes his thumb over my lower lip, a possessive glint in his eyes. "You're the most fascinating creature I've ever known."

Heat floods my cheeks at the compliment. Marcus sees me in a way no one else does, peering beneath the surface to glimpse the hidden depths within. His interest makes me feel cherished, valued in a way I've never experienced before.

I cling to him, overwhelmed by the intensity of my feelings. "What about you?" I venture. "You never talk about your past or your family or..." I trail off, afraid I've overstepped.

But Marcus only smiles, a flicker of vulnerability in his eyes. "My history isn't nearly as interesting as the present." He slides a hand into my hair, tilting my head back. "Or the future I hope to build with you."

My heart stutters at the implication behind his words. "Marcus, I—"

"Shh." He presses a finger to my lips, eyes gleaming. "No more talking. I only want to hear the sounds you make when I touch you."

Our shared heat permeates the small space between us. Marcus' fingers explore the curve of my hip, sending tendrils of desire licking up my spine. His touch is as intoxicating as a fine wine, making my head spin and my body ache for more.

The sensation of his hardened length pressing against me ignites a fire within, stoking an insatiable hunger that only he can sate. I can feel the outline of him through the thin fabric of our clothing, burning hot and begging for release.

His other hand slides up from my waist, tracing a path over the swell of my breasts. His deft fingers skim along the silk barrier before finding their way beneath it, cupping the soft mound with unadulterated possessiveness. The rough pad of his thumb grazes over an already taut nipple, drawing forth a whimper that echoes in the still air around us.

Pinned against him, there's nowhere to hide from the spiraling pleasure coiling in my lower belly. His demanding kiss shatters any remaining reservations I had, setting free a wave of animalistic need that takes control of my senses.

My hands find their way to his belt buckle, fingers fumbling in their haste to rid him of his restricting pants. They fall in a heap at our feet, revealing every inch of his pulsing arousal.

He growls deep in his throat at my bold move, rewarding me with another searing kiss that leaves me breathless. "You're wearing too many clothes," he husks against my lips, nimble fingers working on the buttons of my blouse.

When it joins his discarded trousers on the floor, all that stands between us is a flimsy piece of lace. He hooks one finger under its edge and pulls it down slowly, unveiling me piece by piece. His gaze devours every inch exposed skin like a starving man presented with a feast.

"You're exquisite," he whispers hoarsely, lips dipping to taste the curve of my breast. He laves his tongue over the pebbled flesh before enclosing it with his mouth, suckling with a fervor that sends me spiraling into ecstasy.

His fingers worm their way between our bodies, seeking out the apex of my thighs. I gasp at the first contact, back arching as he dips a finger inside me. The sensation sends jolts of pleasure coursing through me, stoking the fire already raging within. I've touched myself before, but it's never felt like this! It's like Marcus's hands are made of gold.

He crooks his finger, hitting a spot inside me that has me seeing stars. My nails dig into his shoulders as wave after wave of pleasure wracks my body, pushing me closer and closer to the edge of blissful oblivion.

One hand supports my weight while the other works tirelessly to draw forth cries and whimpers from deep within me.

"Marcus!" I scream his name as I shatter, white hot release rushing through me.

With a sweep of his hand, he brushes everything off his desk. Papers flutter to the floor as he lays me on it.

"Motherfucker!" he groans as he moves in between my legs and thrusts deep inside me.

I gasp at the pinch of pain and cling to him.

"Hot damn," he gasps. "Knew this little thing was untapped. You've been saving it for me, haven't you, baby?"

I bury my face in his neck, but he tips my chin up and makes me look at him.

"Don't ever hide from me," he tells me. "I love that you're only mine. No one else will ever touch you this way, Charlotte. Do you understand me?"

Maybe I should be offended by the firm way he issues his order, but instead, it turns me on. My pussy clenches around him as I bite my lip and nod my acquiescence.

"Oh fuck, baby. Trying to kill me with the tight cunt. I gotta move, honey, before I die."

And then he does.

He pulls his hips back and starts barreling into me in strong, powerful thrust. He's hitting this spot deep inside me that feels so good it makes me see stars.

I'm on the verge of something cataclysmic, and I'm whimpering and straining, pushing my hips back against him.

"Yes, that's it, you perfect, perfect girl. Fuck me back. Give it to me," Marcus hisses. He sucks on my neck, and my body quakes.

I know there is no escape from this man or the inferno we've ignited. Each thrust takes us higher and higher until we're both teetering on the precipice, ready to plunge headfirst into shared ecstasy.

"Fuck... Charlotte," he groans my name like a prayer as he drives us relentlessly toward our climax. My body clenches around him, waves of intense pleasure rolling over us as we shatter together.

And I know that I'll never be the same again.

Marcus has buried more than his seed inside my body. He's put a piece of himself inside my heart too.

———

I find myself watching the clock, counting the seconds until Marcus calls. His voice alone is enough to soothe the restless ache inside me, the craving for his presence that never seems to fade.

When he finally summons me to his office, I hurry to obey. He's standing by the window, gazing out at the city below, but he turns at the sound of my footsteps.

Our eyes meet across the room, and for a moment we simply stare at one another. Then he closes the distance between us in three swift strides, pulling me into his arms.

I cling to him, breathing in his familiar scent. "I missed you." The admission slips out before I can stop it.

"Did you?" Marcus tilts my chin up, studying my face. "I want you here with me, Charlotte. Every second of every day." His thumb strokes along my jaw, a possessive caress. "I can't get enough of you."

Joy and trepidation mingle in my chest. I know I should put distance between us, but instead I find myself sinking deeper into his embrace. "I feel the same."

Marcus's eyes darken. "Then stay with me tonight." He nuzzles my neck, lips trailing over sensitive skin. "We don't have to go into the office tomorrow. We can lock the doors and pretend the rest of the world doesn't exist."

My heart pounds at the images flashing through my mind. A secret fantasy come to life, hours alone with Marcus and no one to interrupt us. But this is dangerous territory we're treading, a line we can't uncross.

I open my mouth to refuse, but his name emerges as a sigh instead. "Marcus."

"I need this, Charlotte." His voice is rough with longing. "I need you."

The words melt my resistance, awakening a possessiveness of my own. Marcus is mine, and I'm not ready to share him with the world again just yet.

"Yes," I breathe, sealing my fate with a single word. "Take me home."

A fierce triumph lights Marcus's eyes. He claims my mouth in a searing kiss, and I know I've given him exactly what he craved all along.

Me.

And that knowledge makes me feel special.

Marcus leads me out of the office under cover of darkness, shielding me from prying eyes. By the time we make it to his car, desire has overtaken my senses. I can think of nothing but being alone with him, sating this ravenous hunger that threatens to consume me whole.

We barely make it through the front door of his mansion before he presses me against the wall, mouth descending to claim mine. I arch into him, craving the feel of his hard body against my own.

"Bedroom," he growls, scooping me into his arms. I cling to him as he navigates the sprawling house, kicking open doors until he finds the right one.

When he lowers me to the bed, a thrill courses through me. Marcus prowls above, eyes glowing with predatory heat. I'm caught, willingly ensnared in his web, and I wouldn't have it any other way.

He undresses me with slow, deliberate movements, savoring each new inch of skin revealed. I tremble beneath his gaze, exposed and vulnerable yet utterly unafraid. Marcus won't hurt me. He protects what is his.

"You're exquisite," he rasps, trailing calloused fingers down my body. I arch into his touch, craving more. He obliges, hands and mouth roving across my flesh until I'm writhing against the sheets, incoherent pleas spilling from my lips.

Marcus finally claims again, and I surrender the last remaining shreds of my heart. We move together as one, drowning in pleasure and in each other. Release comes swift and all-consuming, binding us together with invisible threads.

Afterward we lie tangled in each other's arms, sated yet craving more. I know with startling clarity that it will never be enough. I belong to Marcus now, in body and soul, and there's no going back.

———

The next morning, I awaken to the smell of breakfast. I pad down into the kitchen and smile when I see my powerful boss standing over a stove cooking. When he spots me, a lazy smile pulls at his face before he pulls me close and kisses me deeply, uncaring of my disheveled state or the food growing cold on the table behind us. I melt into him, the rest of the world fading away.

We eat between lingering touches and heated gazes, conversation punctuated by the slide of bare feet and the brush of hands. A sense of peace settles over me unlike any I've known before. Here in Marcus's home, wrapped up in his presence, I've found my sanctuary.

The rest of the day passes in a haze of pleasure and contentment. We explore each other unhurriedly, as if we have all the time in the world. And I suppose we do because he's the boss, so I don't have to worry about getting fired.

I smile as he presses another heated kiss to my neck. He's insatiable, and I'm loving every minute of it.

How did I ever get this lucky?

CHAPTER
FIVE

Marcus

I ARRANGE the last silver candlestick and light the wicks, bathing the room in a soft golden glow.

Everything is perfect.

The flames flicker and dance, casting shadows that cling to the walls.

My heartbeat quickens.

Ever since that first day I took her, I can't get enough. It will never be enough. My hands itch with the need to possess, to claim what is mine.

I glance at the velvet box resting on the table, a symbol of my devotion.

And my obsession.

The necklace is a promise. A promise that she will be mine, in body and soul, forever. It doesn't matter that she's given her body to me. It's not enough. I need confirmation that she's *mine*. I'm almost sick with the fear that she could change her mind, that she could leave me.

Forever. The word echoes through my mind, a dark promise of eternal possession.

My gaze drifts to the door, willing it to open.

Needing her to walk through, to see what I have done.

For *her*.

Always for her.

The candles cast a golden glow over the room, but it is her radiance that I crave. Her light, her warmth, her life.

I want to drown in her, to lose myself completely.

She is my drug, my addiction, my *everything*.

Without her, I am nothing.

The door creaks open, and she steps inside, her eyes widening as she takes in the scene before her.

My heart leaps at the sight of her, at the vision of loveliness in the doorway.

"Charlotte," I breathe, the name like a prayer on my lips.

She is beauty personified, my angel, my—

"Marcus, what is all this?" Her voice is a caress, melting my restraint.

I rise and stride toward her, unable to stop myself from reaching out to grasp her hands.

They are soft and warm in my grip, fragile and breakable.

But she is not fragile, my Charlotte. She is strength, she is fire—she is *mine*.

"This is for you," I whisper, raising her hands to my lips. "Everything I do, I do for you."

Her eyes meet mine, blue flames flickering with unease. But there is desire there too, a hunger to match my own.

She wants this as much as I do.

She was made for me, created to complete the dark half of my soul.

Tonight she will accept that truth, and give herself to me.

Wholly, willingly, eternally.

I guide Charlotte to her seat, pulling out her chair for her with a flourish.

She sits, and I lean down to brush my lips against the soft skin of her neck.

Her pulse flutters wildly against my mouth, testament to her arousal.

"Relax, darling," I murmur. "I want this to be a night you will never forget."

I straighten and move to pour her a glass of wine, the deep red liquid shimmering in the candlelight.

The meal I have ordered is laid out before us, multiple courses designed to tantalize the senses.

Luscious foods in a symphony of textures and flavors.

I watch, enthralled, as Charlotte takes her first bite.

A delicate moan escapes her lips, and my body tightens in response.

Tonight I will wring more of those sounds from her, again and again until she is screaming my name.

"This is incredible," she says softly.

I know she does not refer only to the food.

Our connection has always been intoxicating, a drug more potent than the finest wine or any gourmet dish.

"It is merely a taste of the pleasures I wish to give you," I reply, my voice a low promise.

Her eyes flash up to meet mine, dark with unspoken longing.

"Marcus—"

But she does not continue, and I do not need her to.

Her desire is written on her face, in the parting of her lips and the flutter of her lashes.

Tonight she will be mine, in body as well as soul.

I reach across the table to capture her hand, rubbing my thumb slowly over her knuckles.

"Are you enjoying yourself?" I ask softly.

Her tongue darts out to wet her lips and she nods.

"Yes. Very much so."

My pants feel uncomfortably tight, my cock throbbing with need.

I crave the taste of her, the feel of her soft, warm flesh against my own.

The beast rages, clawing to break free, to claim what is his.

Charlotte shifts in her seat, color rising in her cheeks.

She feels it too, this molten heat and aching hunger.

I lean forward, pinning her in place with my stare.

Her lips part but no sound emerges.

I grasp her chin, tilting her head up.

Her eyes are glassy pools that I could drown in.

And finally, I can take it no longer.

I crush my mouth against hers, greedily devouring her soft cries.

My tongue plunges past her lips, tasting, claiming, possessing what is mine.

Her hands fist in my shirt as she melts into the kiss, surrendering herself to me.

Triumph surges within, white hot and primal.

I yank her onto my lap, her thighs straddling my hips.

My hands roam over the curve of her ass, pulling her tighter against my aching cock.

She moans, grinding down on me, hungry and wanton.

I break away from her mouth to nip at her throat, marking her, branding her.

"You're mine," I growl against her skin.

"Yours," she whispers, and I grin.

Our kiss deepens, all teeth and tongue, savage in its intensity.

My hands grip her hips, guiding her movements as she rocks against my straining erection.

Pressure builds within, white hot pleasure tinged with pain, intensifying with each roll of her hips.

I wrench my mouth from hers, panting harshly.

My restraint is fraying, control slipping through my fingers like sand.

I grip her chin, our gazes locking.

"Look at what you do to me." My voice emerges as a snarl.

Her eyes drop and widen at the prominent bulge in my trousers.

A rosy blush stains her cheeks, equal parts embarrassment and feminine pride.

My hand tightens on her chin.

"Look. At. Me."

Her gaze lifts to meet mine once more, blue eyes dark with desire.

"You feel it, don't you?" I hiss. "How much I want you. How deep my hunger goes."

She swallows hard, chest rising and falling with rapid breaths.

I see the moment her resistance crumbles, surrender etched into the lines of her face.

"Yes," she whispers.

Triumph flares within my chest, white hot and blinding.

I crush my mouth to hers once more, claiming what is mine.

Our kiss slows, softening into languid slides of lips and tongue.

I trail my mouth across her jaw, nibbling at her earlobe.

"I have something for you," I murmur.

Her eyes flutter open as I retrieve the velvet box from my pocket.

I flip it open to reveal the diamond necklace within, a symbol of possession and commitment.

"Marcus," she breathes, eyes widening at the extravagant gift.

"You're mine now, in every way that matters." My tone brooks no argument.

"Every way," she echoes softly.

The diamonds wink in the candlelight, a visible claim that marks her as my own.

Satisfaction swells within my chest at the sight.

She is mine, now and forever. No matter the cost.

Charlotte stares down at the necklace, conflicting emotions warring behind her eyes.

Her hands clench into fists where they rest on the table, knuckles turning white under the strain.

I can see the thoughts racing through her mind, weighing desire against danger, passion against prudence.

"You don't approve." My tone is deceptively mild.

She flinches at the accusation, gaze snapping up to meet mine.

"No, that's not—the necklace is beautiful. Extravagant." She worries her lower lip between teeth, hesitating.

"But?" I prompt when she remains silent.

She takes a deep breath, seeming to gather her courage.

"But this, whatever is between us, it's moving so fast. I don't know if I can keep up."

I reach across the table, grasping her hands in my own. Her fingers tremble within my grip.

"There's no need to be afraid." My voice is a low croon, meant to soothe.

"I would never do anything to hurt you."

The words taste like ashes on my tongue. I think of how I've been stalking her, how betrayed she would feel if she knew. I ignore the bitterness.

"We were meant to be together, Charlotte. Can't you feel that?"

She stares at our joined hands, brow furrowing. I give her hands a gentle squeeze.

"I just want you to be sure," she says softly. "Be sure this is what you really want. Before we go any further."

"I have never been more sure of anything in my life."

She searches my face, looking for any sign of deception.

Finding none, her expression softens into a shy, tremulous smile.

"Okay," she whispers. "I'm yours."

Triumph surges within me once more.

"And I am yours," I vow, sealing my promise with a kiss.

She takes the necklace from its velvet cradle, holding it up to examine it in the candlelight.

The platinum chain glints, set with a single diamond that refracts the flickering flames into a dazzling display of color.

"It's beautiful," she breathes, eyes shining with wonder.

I pluck the necklace from her grasp, stepping behind her chair.

"May I?"

She nods, gathering her hair and sweeping it over one shoulder to bare the slender column of her neck.

My fingers brush against her skin as I fasten the clasp, sending a shiver down her spine.

I bend lower, lips grazing the curve of her neck. She sighs softly, head tilting to the side in invitation.

"Exquisite," I murmur against her skin. "The necklace was made for you."

My hands slide over her shoulders, relishing the feel of her silken skin and delicate bones beneath my palms.

"Everything I have will be yours. All you need to do is say yes."

She swallows hard, pulse fluttering wildly against my lips.

"Yes," she whispers. "Yes, Marcus, I'm yours."

Triumph and desire surge within me, an intoxicating blend that threatens to overwhelm my senses.

I straighten, spinning her chair to face me. Her lips part on a gasp as I crush her mouth beneath my own, claiming what now belongs solely to me.

She is mine, at last. And I have no intention of ever letting her go.

Charlotte

I TWIST the brass knob and step into Marcus's dimly lit office, scanning the messy desk for the documents I need.

Hmmm, not here. Maybe he threw them in a drawer?

My fingers graze against...lace? I pause, heart pounding. What is—

No. I jerk my hand back. None of my business.

But curiosity burns through my veins. I glance over my shoulder at the closed door, guilt and longing warring inside me.

With trembling fingers, I reach into the drawer

again. Soft lace caresses my skin. I grasp the fabric and pull.

White lacy panties. No, not just any panties. *Mine.*

The missing pair.

Shock rips through me, sharp as a knife. *Marcus.*

My breaths come fast and shallow. My shaky hand knocks the mouse of the computer, and I notice a file on the desktop with my name on it.

With dread, I click on it. Picture after picture of me. Asleep. It's obvious the cameraman is in my room.

How long has he been watching me? Spying on me like I'm his own personal peep show?

Revulsion curls my stomach. But beneath it lurks a darker feeling. *Excitement.*

I drop the panties as if they've burned me.

I knew he was possessive, even obsessive, but I know just how far it goes.

I have to get out of here. Away from him. But my legs won't move. I'm frozen, torn between fear and something else I don't dare name.

The lace cuts into my palms, but I cling to it like a lifeline. The only thing anchoring me in a world that's spinning out of control.

I stumble out of his office, panties clutched in my fist. The edges of my vision go dark and hazy. I need to get out of here before I pass out, before he comes back and finds me like this.

My legs move on autopilot, carrying me down the hall. Through the lobby, ignoring the curious glances of the receptionist. Out the front doors into the biting wind.

The cold air slaps my face, shocking some of the numbness away. I take a deep, ragged breath that scrapes my raw throat.

Think. I need to think. But my mind is a chaotic swirl of rage and betrayal.

How could he do this? How could I have been so stupid?

The signs were all there. I just didn't want to see them. His intensity, his obsession...the way he looked at me sometimes like he wanted to devour me whole.

I hug myself, panties crumpled in my fist. He already *has* devoured me. Swallowed up the best parts of me and left nothing behind but a shell.

Anger wars with sorrow, twisting my insides into knots. I don't know whether to scream or collapse into tears.

So I do neither. I stand motionless on the sidewalk, buffeted by the wind. Waiting for the maelstrom inside me to quiet so I can figure out where to go from here.

One thing is certain—after today, nothing will ever be the same.

***

My phone buzzes in my pocket again, rattling

against my hip. No doubt another call or text from Marcus.

I don't bother checking. I won't answer. Not now, not ever again.

He's left dozens of increasingly desperate voice-mails and texts over the past couple days. At first pleading, then demanding I return to work. Return to him.

As if.

Does he really think I'm that stupid? That I would willingly subject myself to his manipulation and abuse again?

But I feel a prick of longing when I think of him. I promptly tamp those feelings down, though. I *cannot* be with a man who betrays me.

No matter how much my body still burns for him.

The phone keeps buzzing. I yank it from my pocket and hurl it into the street, watching with grim satisfaction as it shatters under the wheels of a passing taxi.

Let him keep calling. I've cut the lines of communication once and for all.

My hand closes around the panties in my pocket, crumpling the lace and silk into a ball.

I straighten my shoulders against the wind. The storm inside begins to settle into a cold, hard resolve.

It's time to move on. Past the betrayal, past the hurt, past Marcus.

But I feel my resolve crumble even as I think of it, think of never seeing his handsome, face again, never seeing the way his eyes burn when they settle on me.

Tears stream down my cheeks as I head home, each step I put between us making my heart feel heavier.

CHAPTER
SEVEN

Marcus

I SLIP the key into Charlotte's apartment door, the cold metal biting against my skin as I turn it, making sure not to make a sound. My obsession for her has brought me here, in the middle of the night, without her knowing any better. The door creaks open, just enough for me to slip inside.

The darkness envelops me like a cloak, and my heart races with anticipation as I close the door behind me. My breath comes out in short, ragged gasps, betraying my desire to find her, to see her in the sanctity of her own home. I swallow hard, fighting down the knot of anxiety that threatens to consume me.

I move through the darkened apartment, each step calculated and deliberate, my ears straining to catch any sign of her stirring. The air is thick with the scent of her—floral and sweet, intoxicating me further. My need for her grows stronger with every passing second, driving me onward.

My eyes adjust to the faint moonlight filtering through the windows, casting eerie shadows on the walls. I feel like a hunter stalking his prey, and the thought sends a thrill down my spine. This game of cat and mouse excites me, even though I know deep down that it's not a game at all—it's a desperate, all-consuming need that only she can satisfy.

I pause outside her bedroom door, my pulse quickening. The handle turns easily under my grip, and I push the door open, my breath catching in my throat as I step inside.

The moment my eyes land on her, I can't help but let out a barely audible sigh of relief. There she is, lying in the middle of her bed like an angel who's graced me with her presence. The moonlight streams through the curtains, casting a gentle glow upon her delicate features. Charlotte's beauty is ethereal, and it strikes me to my core.

I approach the edge of her bed, treading softly so as not to disturb her slumber. My heart hammers in my chest, threatening to burst from the sheer intensity of the emotions coursing through me. Standing over her, I drink in every detail—the way her chest rises and falls with each breath, the soft curl of her hair against her cheek, and the peaceful expression on her face.

"Fuck," I whisper under my breath, unable to tear my gaze away from her. My desire for her intensifies exponentially, consuming my every thought and fueling my obsession.

"Charlotte," I murmur, almost involuntarily, as if speaking her name will somehow tether me to this moment, to her. "You have no idea what you do to me."

My eyes trace the curve of her body beneath the thin sheets, and I harden. I want to run my hands along her skin, to taste her lips, to claim her as my own again. The raw hunger gnawing at me is overpowering, driving me to the brink of madness, yet I fight against it, knowing that I must savor this moment for as long as possible.

"God, I need you," I confess, my voice barely more than a whisper.

I take a step back, my body trembling with the effort to maintain control. Every cell in my being screams for me to close the distance between us once again, to make her mine in the most primal and possessive way imaginable.

But instead I watch her, my erection making an obsence tent in my pants as I torture myself.

———

Charlotte

An icy shiver races down my spine, and I sense that something is off. My eyes flutter open to find Marcus's dark gaze locked on me, the intensity of his stare burning through the darkness. For a second, I can't breathe, as if the air in the room has grown thick with tension.

"Wh-what are you doing here?" I stammer, my voice barely audible. Panic rises within me, threatening to swallow me whole.

"Shh," he murmurs, his voice low and commanding. "Don't be scared, Charlotte."

I scramble to sit up, clutching the sheets to my chest with trembling hands. My heart hammers in my chest, and I can't help but wonder how we reached this point. How did I end up here, with him—the man whose desires both terrify and intrigue me?

"Marcus, please... You shouldn't be here," I whisper, my voice shaking, but he doesn't seem to hear me.

"God, you're beautiful," he breathes, his eyes roving over my body hungrily, leaving a trail of heat in their wake. "You have no idea what you do to me, Charlotte."

"Please... leave," I plead, my voice barely a whisper. But deep down, I know he won't go—not when I've given him a taste of what he craves.

And...do I really want him to? My indecision scares me.

"Can't you see it, Charlotte?" Marcus asks, his voice laced with need. "The way you affect me? The way you've burrowed under my skin?"

I struggle to keep my breathing steady, fear and desire warring within me. I've never felt so exposed, so vulnerable in my life. And yet, there's something intoxicating about the raw hunger in his eyes, the way they consume me whole.

"Marcus..." I murmur, unable to tear my gaze away from his.

"Say it again," he commands, his voice a dark seduction. "Say my name like you want me, like you need me."

"Marcus," I whisper, the sound of his name on my lips a forbidden pleasure I can't deny myself. And now I know, right or wrong, there's no turning back now.

"Good girl," he murmurs, his voice rough with desire. "Now, let me show you what it means to be mine."

My heart hammers in my chest as I watch Marcus's

eyes darken, his voice trembling with a mix of desperation and adoration. "Charlotte, I love you," he confesses, baring his soul to me without any hesitation. "I've loved you since the moment I laid eyes on you. You're my obsession, my everything."

I can't help but shiver at the intensity of his words, fear and desire coiling together in my gut like a living thing. Every instinct tells me to run, to escape his smoldering gaze, but there's something in his vulnerability that holds me captive.

"Please, don't be afraid," he pleads, his eyes searching mine for any sign of understanding. "I know how this must look, but I swear, all I want is to protect you, to cherish you. I'd do anything for you, Charlotte."

His words wash over me like a tidal wave, drowning out the small voice of reason that still lingers in the back of my mind. It's terrifying, this strange pull he has over me, how easily he can make my heart race with just a few whispered words.

"Marcus," I whisper, my voice barely audible above the pounding of my heart. "I... I don't know what to say."

"Say you'll let me in," he implores, desperation leaking into his voice. "Let me show you just how much I care for you."

My breath catches in my throat, torn between the urge to give in to his dark allure and the fear of losing myself completely to his desires. But deep down, I know that no matter what choice I make, I'm already lost. I'm irrevocably bound to him by a twisted web of lust and obsession.

"Okay," I breathe, my body trembling with anticipation.

"Charlotte," Marcus warns, his voice low and dangerous, "you need to understand something. You'll never be free of me." His eyes burn with intensity, the heat of his gaze searing into me as if to brand me as his own. "I will always be there, watching you, desiring you, controlling your every move."

My breath hitches in my chest, but instead of feeling suffocated by his words, I feel an unexpected thrill coursing through my veins. My body responds to his possessiveness with a strange sense of liberation, as if he's unlocked a hidden part of myself that has been yearning for this level of control.

"Marcus, I..." My voice falters, unable to articulate the storm of emotions raging inside me.

"Shh," he whispers, placing a finger against my lips. "You don't need to say anything, Charlotte. Just know that I'm always with you, even when you think you're alone."

His touch sends shivers down my spine, and I can't help but lean into it. The darkness of his desire wraps around me like a cocoon, both comforting and constricting. And as much as I fear what this connection might mean for us, I can't deny the allure of his dominance.

"Show me," I plead, desperate for him to reveal the depths of our twisted bond. "Show me how far this goes."

A slow, predatory smile curves Marcus's lips as he reaches out to brush a strand of hair from my face. His fingers trail down my cheek, sending goosebumps rippling across my skin.

"Good girl," Marcus praises me as he leans in to press a lingering kiss to my forehead. "You know we were always meant to be."

As Marcus moves closer, I feel the warmth radiating from his body. The distance between us narrows until there is nothing left but trembling breaths and the pounding of our hearts.

"Charlotte," he whispers, his voice rough with desire as his fingers tangle in my hair, pulling me toward him. "I need you."

"Marcus," I breathe, my own need matching his intensity.

Our lips crash together in a desperate, consuming kiss, his tongue exploring the depths of my mouth with a hunger that leaves me breathless. Hands roam over fevered skin, greedily claiming every curve, every secret hollow. This is not a gentle joining. It is a declaration of possession, an unyielding demand for submission that I cannot deny.

"Tell me," he growls against my ear, biting down on the tender flesh as a shudder of pleasure courses through me. "Tell me you're mine."

"I'm yours," I gasp, lost in the whirlwind of sensation and emotion that threatens to consume us both. "Always."

"Good," he murmurs, his voice thick with satisfaction as he draws back to stare into my eyes. "Because I love you. I fucking love you to the point of madness."

The words hang heavy in the air, charged with a darkness that neither of us can escape. And yet, as I gaze into the depths of his soul, I see the truth of his confession mirrored in the raw vulnerability that lingers just beneath the surface.

"I love you too," I admit, my voice shaking with the weight of this newfound revelation. "I don't understand it, but I do."

"Love isn't meant to be understood," he tells me, his lips brushing against mine in a searing promise of all that we will become. "It's meant to be felt."

And as our bodies entwine, lost in the shared madness of our desires, I can't help but feel that this love—dark and twisted though it may be—is the one thing that will truly set us free.

As Marcus's lips leave mine, our chests heave in

unison, the room now a battleground of tangled limbs and whispered moans. I feel his hands on my bare skin, their touch rough yet tender, leaving trails of fire in their wake. My nails dig into his shoulders, urging him to bring me closer to the edge of oblivion.

"Fuck, Charlotte," Marcus groans, his voice strained as he nips at my neck. "Fuck, fuck, fuck, baby. I gotta get inside you, honey."

"Then take me. I'm yours," I breathe.

Marcus doesn't hesitate, flipping me onto my back with a predatory glint in his eyes. He looms over me, his strong frame casting a shadow that feels both terrifying and thrilling. The air is thick with the scent of sweat and desire, as though we are creating our very own storm within these four walls.

"Fuck, you're perfect," he murmurs, trailing his fingers down my spine, eliciting a shudder of pleasure from me. His touch is everywhere. It's all-consuming and intoxicating, making it impossible to think about anything other than the present moment.

He spears himself into me, and I scream in both pleasure and pain as he groans, a deep, guttural sound of male satisfaction.

"Marcus," I gasp, feeling the tension coil tighter inside me as our bodies move in perfect synchrony. "Please... I need more."

"Tell me what you want," he demands, his voice low and commanding. "I'll give you anything, baby."

"Harder," I whimper, meeting his intense gaze. "Take me like you own me."

"Fuck, yes," he growls, his grip on my hips tightening as he thrusts into me with renewed force. The pain mixes with pleasure, and I can't help but scream, the sound raw and primal as it echoes through the room.

"Mine," he repeats between ragged breaths, his words searing themselves into my very soul. "You're fucking *mine*, Charlotte."

"Yours," I agree, lost in the heady rush of surrender as our connection deepens with every touch, every gasp, and every shared moment of ecstasy. "Only yours, Marcus."

As our bodies collide, driven by the darkness that binds us together, I can't help but wonder if this is what freedom feels like—the sweet, unyielding embrace of desire, dominance, and control.

As the last remnants of our primal dance fade into the darkness, my body trembles with exhaustion, yet my mind races with the intensity of the night's events. Marcus' strong arms wrap around me, pulling me against his chest as we lay tangled in sweat-soaked sheets. His breath is heavy and hot against my neck, each exhale a testament to the passion we've just shared.

"Fuck, Charlotte," he whispers, his voice laced with both awe and satisfaction. "That was...I can't even find the words."

"Neither can I," I admit, struggling to catch my breath. My heart pounds wildly in my chest, still reeling from the depths of desire we've explored together. As Marcus' fingers trace lazy circles on my skin, the sensation sends shivers down my spine, reminding me that my body remains hungry for his touch.

"Is this really what you want?" he asks, a hint of vulnerability seeping into his tone. The question hangs heavy in the air, threatening to shatter the fragile peace that surrounds us.

"Marcus," I breathe, turning my head to meet his smoldering gaze. "It scares me, but yes, it's what I want. It's what I need."

"Good," he murmurs, leaning down to press a possessive kiss against my lips. "Because I'm not letting you go, Charlotte. Not ever."

"Promise?" I ask, my voice barely audible above the pounding of my heart.

"Cross my fucking heart," he swears, tightening his embrace around me as if to prove his point. His words are like a balm to my soul, easing the fear that had been gnawing at the edges of my mind.

"Then let's sleep," I whisper, snuggling closer to his warmth, seeking comfort in the knowledge that he's here, that he's mine. For better or worse, our obsessions have bound us together, and there's no turning back now.

"Sleep," he agrees, his eyes sliding shut as his body gradually relaxes. I feel the rhythm of his breath slowly becoming steady, signaling that he's drifting off to sleep.

As I surrender to the pull of slumber, my thoughts drift to the uncharted territory that lies ahead. We've crossed a line tonight, and there's no going back. Our desires, so dark and all-consuming, will forever bind us together, for better or worse. And yet, as I listen to Marcus' steady heartbeat beneath my ear, I can't help but feel a strange sense of peace.

"Goodnight, Marcus," I whisper into the darkness, finally allowing myself to succumb to the sweet oblivion of sleep, knowing that my love and obsession for this man will be both my salvation and my undoing.

EPILOGUE

Three Years Later

Charlotte

THE OFFICE IS DIMLY LIT, the air heavy with passion and longing. I sit at my desk, stealing glances at Marcus as he pores over legal documents, his brow furrowed in concentration.

His eyes flick up, meeting my gaze, and a slow smile spreads across his lips. "Come here, Charlotte."

His voice is low and rough, sending a shiver of anticipation down my spine. I rise and cross the room, perching on the edge of his desk. His hands grasp my waist, pulling me onto his lap.

"You've been distracting me all day. Shouldn't you be writing?" he murmurs, his breath hot against my neck. I gasp as his teeth graze my skin, desire pooling low in my belly.

"I can't help it." My words come out breathless. "You're the one who insisted we share an office."

A low chuckle rumbles in his chest. "And now I'm going to insist you make it up to me." His hands slide under my skirt, fingers digging into my thighs. I moan, arching into his touch.

The familiar ache builds within me as his hands explore my body, each caress heightening my need for him. Only he can satisfy me this way, bring me to the brink of madness and ecstasy all at once.

"You're mine," he growls, roughly claiming my mouth. I melt into the kiss, surrendering myself to him completely. I *am* his, body and soul, and there is no place I'd rather be.

I got my degree, and then I went on to become a bestselling author. Marcus is still a billionaire executive, but he never goes in to the office anymore. He works out of a home office now because he can't bear to be away from me.

That's fine by me. I write romance novels, and what we do on our "breaks" in our office provides me with plenty of inspiration.

Our desire for each other is ravenous, insatiable,

all-consuming. But beneath the passion lies a profound devotion—one that transcends lust and physical pleasure. What we share is more than a fleeting romance.

It is a bond beyond all earthly limits, eternal as the tides.

Marcus tears his mouth from mine, eyes dark with desire. "On the desk. Now."

His commanding tone sends a thrill through me. I scramble onto the desk, heart pounding as he prowls toward me. There's a predatory gleam in his eyes, a hunger that threatens to devour me whole.

He grabs my legs and yanks me to the edge of the desk. "You're mine to do with as I please." His hands slide under my skirt again, roughly pushing my panties aside. "And I fully intend to please myself with you."

I gasp as two fingers plunge deep inside me. Marcus sets a punishing rhythm, his grip bruising my thighs. The ache grows unbearable, pleasure and pain twisting together. I cry out, unable to form words, lost in the sensations he evokes.

"Who do you belong to?" he demands.

"You," I moan. "Only you."

A smile curves his lips. He adds another finger, stretching me, stoking the fire within. "That's right. You're mine, Charlotte, now and forever." His thumb presses against my clit, pushing me to the brink. "Come for me. Show me you're mine."

The climax crashes over me in a blinding wave. I scream his name, clinging to his shoulders as the pleasure ravages my body. Through the haze of ecstasy, I'm dimly aware of Marcus murmuring words of love and devotion. His touch is both possessive and tender, staking his claim while soothing me in the aftermath of release.

Then I gasp as Marcus enters me in one swift thrust, filling me to the hilt. The slight pain only intensifies my pleasure, the evidence of his possession. He pulls back slowly, watching me with hooded eyes, before driving into me again.

"So tight," he groans. "So perfect." His fingers dig into my hips as he sets a brutal pace, pounding into me. I cry out, clinging to his shoulders, lost in the primal rhythm of our joining.

Marcus ducks his head, teeth grazing my throat, a silent threat and promise. I tilt my head back in submission, baring my neck in invitation. He growls deep in his chest, biting down on the tender flesh, hard enough to leave his mark.

The sharp sting sends a jolt of electricity through me. "Marcus," I moan, desire coiling hot and heavy in my belly. He sucks at the bruise, tongue flickering over the sensitive skin, even as he continues to thrust inside me.

"Mine," he rasps, raising his head to capture my lips in a searing kiss. His hands slide under my back, crushing me against him, our bodies moving as one.

The warmth spreads through my veins, an inferno raging out of control. Marcus breaks the kiss, resting his forehead against mine, our harsh breaths mingling. His eyes blaze into mine, dark and fathomless, reflecting the depth of his passion.

"Come for me, Charlotte." His voice is a low rasp, ragged with need. "Show me you're mine."

The coil snaps, ecstasy flooding my senses. I cry out his name, clinging to him as the climax shatters me into a thousand pieces, all of them his. Marcus follows soon after, burying his face in my neck with a hoarse shout, his body going taut as he finds his release.

We remain locked in our embrace, hearts pounding against each other's chests. No words are needed in this moment of perfect understanding. us strokes his hands down my back in a gentle caress, his touch reverent. I lift my head from his shoulder to find his gaze trained on me, dark eyes filled with tenderness.

"You're the only thing that matters to me," he whispers, brushing a lock of hair from my face. His words send a thrill through me, even now when our desire has been sated. "The only thing I want, the only thing I need."

I cup his cheek, tracing the line of his jaw. "As you are to me."

This is why we decided not to have children. Yes, children would be a special part of both of us, but Marcus is so possessive of me, he can't bear to share me.

Even with our child.

"I love the thought of breeding you," he told me when we talked about it, "but I don't want to share you. That's how obsessed I am with you."

And I'm okay with that.

A flicker of vulnerability crosses his face at my admission before he captures my mouth in a searing kiss. I can feel the depths of his love and passion pouring into me, a whirlwind of intensity that threatens to sweep me away.

When we finally break apart, breathless, I rest my head over his heart again, listening to its steady beat. His arms tighten around me.

Safe and warm in his embrace, I drift off to sleep, our hearts and souls intertwined.

———

I wake to soft kisses along my neck and shoulders, Marcus's hands roaming over my body. Heat blooms under his touch, desire kindling anew.

"Again?" I ask breathlessly as his mouth finds that sensitive spot below my ear.

"I can never get enough of you." His voice is rough with need. "You're my addiction, Charlotte, my obsession."

I roll over to face him, pressing myself against his hard body. "Then take your fill."

A growl rumbles in his chest as he claims my lips in a searing kiss. Our tongues dance together, stoking the flames of longing. My hands explore the planes of his chest, reveling in the feel of taut muscle under warm skin.

Marcus shifts above me, one hand sliding between my thighs. I gasp into his mouth as he strokes me, plea-sure rippling outwards.

"So wet for me already," he murmurs against my lips. "You want this as much as I do."

"Yes." I arch into his touch, chasing the exquisite sensations. "Marcus, please..."

With a low chuckle, he gives me what I crave, thrusting deep. A strangled moan escapes my throat at the delicious stretch and fullness.

Marcus sets a slow, thorough pace, pulling back until only the tip remains before sinking into me again.

Each stroke awakens nerve endings, building the tension inside.

My nails dig into his back as the tempo increases, broken cries spilling from my lips. The world narrows to just the two of us, all else fading away.

Release comes in a blinding surge of ecstasy, shattering my senses. Marcus follows soon after, burying his face in my neck with a guttural groan.

I love this man. Wholly. Completely. And I'm content to spend every day for the rest of our lives just like this.

Want a free book? Go to www.authoremmabray.com.